Tetra Batair, grandson of Neptune himself and guardian of the god's military forces, has arrived in Charleston, South Carolina for his mate. The only problem? His mate doesn't want him. Now what's a merman to do?

Aoki Tatsuo, an art teacher who's half dragon and half human, doesn't want to be anyone's mate. Or, at least that's what he's telling himself.

When the two first meet the earth trembles... literally.

A merman and a dragon.

One will have to learn patience.

The other will have to learn there's more than one way to love.

Can the two of them work through the obstacles in their past to find their perfect future?

The Guardian's Prize
Copyright © 2018 Deja Black
ISBN: 978-1-4874-2020-8
Cover art by Erin Dameron-Hill

Published by eXtasy Books Inc or
Devine Destinies, an imprint of eXtasy Books Inc

Look for us online at:
www.eXtasybooks.com or www.devinedestinies.com

THE GUARDIAN'S PRIZE
MEN OF NEPTUNE, BOOK 2

BY

DEJA BLACK

DEDICATION

For my children who support me without fail. Mommy's following her dream. May you do the same.

CHAPTER ONE

Tetra Batair walked from the ocean into the darkness of the night, feet stepping beyond the froth of the sea. The waters released him, but not without his promise to return after he'd found his mate. The humans here would know him as Batair, just as his family and men in the ocean did.

He felt his mother's love in the ocean's kiss, her wishes for him to have a prosperous journey and acquire what he sought. He embraced her love and that of his siblings as his skin touched the cooling sand. His youngest brother Trillian's laughter, his sister Calypso's hugs, and the blessing from his entire guardian pod, all eager for his return home. He was their leader, after all, and the benefit of any children his mate produced would add to the pod, strengthening Father Neptune's forces.

When his mother approached Father Neptune to plead for his journey, permission had not been attained without trepidation. Batair was not trained in the life of a human, had not explored as others did—each with tales of the world above the ocean's surface.

What would a visit to the land of hard earth and bitter air of the human world do to a guardian who needed his strength for times of battle? How would time beyond the ocean's depth change him? But his mother was nothing if not a warrior when it came to the happiness of her own children. Especially when she'd been cast away so brutally by her first mate—her true mate.

Batair's mother, Mazu, loved a human who denied their

1

mating and broke her heart. His oldest brother Kamau's father, Jonah Anderson, had called her a monster and abandoned her knowing she was pregnant with his child.

Mazu had put aside her own needs and pain to allow Kamau to have a relationship with his father. She'd requested that Jonah allow Kamau to spend time with him, which hadn't been good for father or son—no matter how Kamau had tried. His father had only used Kamau's siren voice to increase the membership of his church and then threatened to kill the man Kamau loved. When Kamau had to hurt his own father to save his mate, Father Neptune stepped in and denied reentry into the human world for any of his people.

It took years, but she'd finally acquired the release for Batair, so he could search for his mate.

He knew his mate was here. He felt his presence on the land, the place from where his brother Kamau's mate had come. He felt the tremor in the ocean, the ripples in the current as they found him, taking his breath away. His heart raced with the joy of it, heat blazing through his soul and his elustra rising quickly, heedless of the distance. There were those below who sensed his elustra, who pleaded for him to give them his seed to add to the guardian pod, but he would not. His mate waited, and he would not betray him.

He stood naked on the beach, water sluicing down his human skin gifted to him by Father Neptune. Squinting his eyes to the brightness of the moon, he looked for the humans Kamau promised would be waiting for him. After Father Neptune granted his release, all moved quickly to help Batair. Kamau and Graham visited the surface and met with David and Louis, who helped to pave the way for Batair. Batair would have a home, a place to work, and the time he needed to locate his mate.

Looking around, he took a moment to breathe in the air and pushed the ocean water from his gills. Once, twice, and again until his body had adjusted. He felt when his gills shrank into mere slivers that one would have to scrutinize carefully to find. The tiny fins at his ankles were the only sign of his tail.

It wasn't long before two shadows strode down the sands on the path toward him. The smaller one's eyes were wide as he looked over Batair, like a sea lion looking at a penguin for its next meal. He even licked his lips.

"Well, I heard you would be big, but I had no idea how big. You, darling, are massive. Look at those arms and legs." The man—who Batair assumed was David from Kamau's description—breathed deeply and let out a humming sound.

Batair could smell his arousal from where he stood, with the ocean water dancing around his heels, almost like it was afraid to let him go.

"I'm right here, David," Louis said. David's mate was taller than him, broader, but nowhere near the size of a guardian. He didn't appear to be angered by his smaller mate's words. If anything, he smiled warmly at David before kissing him on his cheek.

"I know, baby." David lifted for Louis's kiss and turned back to Batair. "We brought clothing for you and a towel. Hope the clothing fits." His brown eyes perused Batair's body once more, slowly lingering over Batair's dick. "All of you."

"I am a guardian, bred to protect our Father Neptune, little human. My body serves our Father's purpose." It was his role, his destiny since his birth. Everything on him was sizable, including the focus of David's attention.

David smiled but handed over the towel, which Batair used quickly to remove the salty seawater from his body. Next, David passed over the clothes. Batair held up the pants, the shorts, the t-shirt, and the flexible shoes with straps he assumed were to allow the flesh to breathe.

"I'd help you with that, but Louis wouldn't be pleased." That didn't stop his sly smile, though. Batair shook his head.

"No, David. Louis would not," his mate said, his tone calm, hiding no anger or concern.

Batair laughed. He looked down at himself and smiled back at David. "You appreciate what Father Neptune has blessed me with. My body pleases you?" He stepped forward and returned the towel to David, then began putting on the clothing, discarding the short pants. Why would anyone need two of them? One was enough.

"You're going to appreciate having that pair of boxer briefs there to reduce the chafing of your pleasing parts my husband appears to admire so much. I would suggest you put those on," advised Louis.

Batair looked at Louis for a moment, nodded and put the boxer briefs, as he called them, on first. The fabric was soft against him, much different than the armor he wore hewn from coral seabeds and reinforced with shells, the proper attire of a guardian.

"Oh, yes, most certainly. You'll make whoever your mate is one happy man," David responded, his eyes on Batair as he struggled with the shorts.

Interested in seeing what David would do next, he moved to stand in his space only to hear Louis's breathing change. As for David, he moved closer to his mate, easing his fingers into Louis's own.

"Don't worry, human... Louis. I will not attempt to take your mate no matter how pleasing he is to the eye. I am here for my own." Batair moved back and was amused to see how the couple relaxed together. David was a lemon shark, playful and friendly with a potential to be dangerous, but he adored his mate, as Batair could well see.

Batair finished dressing, pulling at the top and the pants. He would have to find clothing suitable for him, as these were snug. Kamau had shared places with him where that might be possible. It would be one of the first things on his list of tasks.

"How do you even know he's here?" Louis asked. He handed Batair a strap of leather indicating he should put them through the sections of cloth on the pants. He thanked him.

"I felt the pulse of the ocean the moment he touched the water. He is here in this place, and I will find him. And I am beholden to your mate and to you for making this possible." Batair bowed respectfully. "Now, I have traveled many leagues to arrive here and must rest before I start my search."

"We're glad to help," Louis said as they turned to leave the shore.

"We most certainly are. How are Graham and Kamau?" David asked, and Batair could hear the concern in his voice. Graham and David were very much like brothers, Batair knew. Graham talked about David often, so he knew how much David missed him.

"Graham is pregnant with their fourth child, so they are both happy. Kamau dotes on him, ensuring that he has everything he could ever need or want. My mother is often at their home visiting with her grandchildren and assisting in their training."

David shook his head. "Graham pregnant? That still surprises me. Kamau shares the images of their family with both of us, and Louis and I couldn't imagine what that's like. But Graham is happy?" he asked, the sincerity in his tone doing much to add to Batair's respect for him.

"My brother's mate smiles and laughs and raises his children. If he were any happier, the sun would shine from within the ocean instead." Batair heard the wistfulness in his own tone. He wanted what his brother had with Graham, the happiness, and children who would later serve as guardians. He had that chance here. He could feel it.

CHAPTER TWO

"Mr. Tatsuo," Elizabeth Ann McCormick said, her eyes sad and the beautiful smile she often wore missing, "There are only two more hours, and school will be out."

Aoki Tatsuo's thoughts wondered as he put away the materials in his art room and prepared for his next class. *Actually, it's one hour forty-five minutes and fifty-one seconds.*

One more class and he was done, then he along with his one-hundred-twenty art students, as well as the rest of Marshall Academy, would enjoy the summer vacation free of worries. No stress of incomplete homework, parent-teacher conferences, or twenty-minute lunch periods. He could even visit the restroom anytime he wished without the threat of a bladder infection or stomach cramps from trying to see if he could trap the Atlantic Ocean in the center of his pelvis.

Ocean water, completing murals—the legalized *tagging* he now worked instead of finding abandoned buildings that served as the canvas to show the world his artwork years ago. And rest and trips into the mountains. He sighed.

In one hour forty-three minutes and fifteen seconds.

"Yes, Elizabeth. A little less than two hours, and you're out of here!"

And me, too.

Instead of Elizabeth smiling at his words, he could see her frown deepening. Pausing at putting the oils back in the right spot once again, he turned to face her.

"Elizabeth?" Aoki asked.

The pint-sized dynamo sighed as if preparing for battle. "I

just want you to know that you're the only reason I'm going to miss Marshall. My parents are splitting up, and with my mom not being able to live here and work at the new job she had to take, I'm going to be leaving Charleston. We're packing up over the summer."

Well, that was a blow. Of the many students Aoki taught, he enjoyed Elizabeth the most. She was a child who craved attention and praise, who didn't just complete a project but dedicated herself to see it shine. She was never absent, sick or not. He would miss her.

Inwardly, his dragon shifted at his discomfort. Never one to allow him to suffer alone, he felt the waves of flame ease him, warming him from the inside, attempting to cleanse him of the pain. Aoki did not handle loss well. He never had. And for him, losing Elizabeth was another reminder of the gap where love should have been. Perhaps if he had his own child, his own family, but it was not to be.

"I'm sorry to hear that, Elizabeth." He truly was. She had talent, promise, and he hoped to help to cultivate that.

"Yeah, I was, too. You know my mom needs looking after, and since Dad can't do it anymore, that leaves me. Someone has to be there for my little brothers."

And that was the crux of it all. No ninth-grade child should have to shoulder the burdens Elizabeth carried. Her mother's mental illness that resulted in her self-medicating with drugs and alcohol did not make Barbara McCormick a suitable homemaker. Once again, Aoki wished he could help Elizabeth, could give her a home where she could just be a kid and allow the developing skills of the prodigious artist she could become to flourish and grow.

Instead, he opened his arms, and she reached around his waist hugging him tightly. His dragon purred inside and would have huffed louder, but he quieted him and hugged Elizabeth back just as tight. No matter how much he wished it, the little girl was not his to keep or a treasure for his dragon.

"You can always email me or send me a text through the class app. I won't delete you."

She pulled back then and sniffed, her eyes wet with tears. Nodding she said, "Yes. Okay, I can do that."

Then, just like nothing had happened at all, she turned and walked away.

There were so many children like her, children who needed a safe place, but Aoki didn't have the den to care for them all.

That didn't stop him from wishing for his own. He turned back to the oils.

When the bell rang, Aoki wiped off his hands and headed towards the door to greet his last class for the day. It went by fast. This time there were no tight hugs, no tears from a broken heart. No, this group made all the melancholy of the coming summer vanish.

Students thought they were the only ones ready for vacation. When Zach Morris aimed a tube of red paint at Felicia Chastain like it was a machine gun, and fired, Aoki was so done, and so ready for the summer break.

Felicia went home thirty minutes early with her hair a garish scarlet red and muddied brown. So, no, he didn't hesitate, didn't slow the process of getting out of school that day. In fact, Aoki was sure he might have helped one child or ten gather their materials faster just to get them out of the room. Yes, he had one more day as a teacher to turn in his keys and suffer through a final school celebration, but he was free. He could travel into the Blue Ridge Mountains to release his dragon. Finish his community projects. Paint. He was free.

Both he and his dragon were more than pleased. Then his cell phone rang, and he saw his mother's number on the caller ID. What did she want? He sensed it, knew there was something brewing, but he had no idea what. His dragon twitched nervously in agreement. If his mother called, she needed him. Summer vacation would have to wait.

Aoki headed to Sisters Three, the restaurant his mother, Bridget, and her two sisters owned. She'd asked him to come immediately after painting today, saying she had a task for him. When he'd asked what needed to be done, his mother told him that it was nothing too great he couldn't handle. But she never once said what it was. Knowing her, it could be anything, and that was what worried him.

Aoki parked his car near his mother's, a Mini Cooper that was painted in rainbow colors. It would be hard not to notice it, which was her intent. He looked at the restaurant, braving himself for whatever unknown machinations his mother had in store.

Sisters Three was surrounded by ancient oak trees, some as big as the Angel Oak Tree near Johns Island, and just as mighty. It was the perfect place for his mother's coven, steeped in history, the earth's magic gathering here. Aoki felt it every time he visited, the lines of power that vibrated in the atmosphere.

His mother's restaurant sat near the coast, the building itself like one of the many colonial homes in the area, teal and white. The colors changed at her whim, sometimes green and coral, other times ivory and beige. Inside there would be rich woods and antique furniture. Beyond that, whatever adornment suited his mother and his aunts' fancy. With summer, the one thing he could count on would be white candles and blossoms kissed by the sun decorating the tables, music playing from a time gone by—the sounds of home.

Stepping out of the car, Aoki placed his foot on the

ground only to have the earth shift the second he touched it. Shaken, he fell back against his car. His dragon stirred, searching, alert and ready. *That was different.*

"What the fuck?" Aoki groaned. When he felt he could move, Aoki searched the area around him. He raised his nose to the air and sniffed, drawing in a scent he didn't recognize but couldn't resist. It drew Aoki further, pulling him along. He had to find it, discover its source. His dragon uncurled within, pressing against the surface, restless and eager. His wings beat beneath his shoulder blades, prepared to capture the origin of the scent and carry it off. Whatever it was, his dragon desired it, and from the direction it was drifting, the intended treasure was in Sisters Three.

CHAPTER THREE

Batair's head lifted from the menu. He had no idea what any of this was, and none of it interested him. He'd only come here because of Kamau's insistence last night when they'd opened the circle.

"You must visit his world, learn the place he's from before you pull him from everything he knows," Kamau *said as he held his youngest, Narin, rocking back and forth. Graham was resting in the background.*

"How is Graham? He looks tired," Batair said while turning over in the large bed — nothing like the one at home, layered in kelp. And though Graham and Kamau's human dwelling was probably quieter than most, the foreign and shrill sounds of cars and machines made him restless. Instead, he longed for the home he saw through the circle, the opening in one of the walls giving way to a view of the ocean, a bed of coral in the distance, a school of fish swimming beyond.

Graham slept on. Graham was good for Kamau, the way he made him smile, Kamau's songs no longer mournful and broken but full of the devotion he shared with the man he loved. This last pregnancy had been rough for them both, the baby heftier than the others, fierce and strong, his tiny body already showing the structure of a guardian. The nurturer had stayed longer with them, using her power to return Graham's strength, repairing the damage the beautiful Narin had left behind.

A guardian? How was that even possible? Only guardians produced guardians. It had always been the way, but there was no denying that his nephew was a guardian. It was there in the

12

makeup of his body. Already, his eyes were open, his powerful fists ready to fight.

Was it Graham, himself, that was the cause? There was something different about the man, the way he fit in seamlessly as part of the world beneath the ocean surface. Was it because he'd been a soldier? Father Neptune had gifted him and Kamau with a place filled with air, sealed off from the ocean. Graham hardly needed it, though, his bond with Kamau strong enough to allow him to live comfortably as their people did.

Kamau looked at his mate as he slept. "He is better, resting more, almost his usual self."

Narin stretched then, his wail loud, the walls trembling as he roared his frustration. Graham woke and opened his arms to take his son. Kamau leaned forward and placed Narin in his father's arms, and the youngling quieted instantly and fell asleep. Graham drifted off, a tired smile on his lips. Kamau sighed. It was evident that his brother was just as tired as his mate.

"What of the other young?"

"All resting. Narin would not be comforted. He's our little warrior and finds strength in being with Graham. The others play and sing and learn their lessons. Not our Narin. He is ready for something more." Kamau stood and pressed against the barrier to their home, swimming into the sea. "Enough about us. Stop trying to distract me."

"I'm not."

"You are, Tetra Batair. Now, tomorrow, I want you to visit Bridget. I will send you the way, and you will go there. Socialize."

"I want —"

"I know what you want, but to find your mate, you will have to live life differently. Your mate is human. Interact with humans."

"Graham and I have interacted," Batair responded.

"Not enough, brother. Now, I'm going back in to rest with my mate and our youngest."

"So far," Batair laughed.

"I don't know. This last breeding, Batair." Kamau shivered.

"You know he wants more children. Your mate is happiest with

his growing family."

"I know."

"And once Father Neptune learns of the birth of a guardian from a human and merman bond?"

"I know. I know."

"Already, he is stronger than even the last guardian at his age."

Kamau groaned in frustration.

"I'm sorry, brother," Batair said. He was sorry, but he couldn't hold back his excitement at an increase in the Guardian line. The possibilities.

"It's no matter. It's true, but this isn't the time for me to dwell on what Father Neptune will want. My heart and mind are with my mate. You will go to Sisters Three. You will meet the three women there who helped me survive, and you will learn what it is your mate needs."

So, Batair sat in Sisters Three, with a menu in hand listing foods that he knew nothing of, surrounded by scents that flooded his mind... and humans. Everywhere. Okay, perhaps not everywhere. There were a few scattered at different tables lit with candles, the fire of the human world potent in its dangerous beauty.

As soon as he'd entered, a beautiful woman whose visage rivaled that of any siren female stood before him and invited him in. Her hair was bone white and fell in three coiling braids down her back. The colors of her clothing were vivid and brilliant, challenging the sea's coral gardens. Her eyes were golden, the sun's own light captured in her orbs.

"Guardian Tetra Batair, welcome to Sisters Three."

Batair stepped back, surprised at hearing his full title. He would have reached for his absent triton, ready to defend himself, because there was no question that this woman was powerful. It flowed from her, easily detected by anyone sensitive to its presence. The way she gripped his forearm, arresting his movements, stilled his breath, but only warmth poured through, warm and searching energy similar to his mother's.

"How? What?"

"Peace, beautiful one. I am Bridget. Kamau and I spoke, and I wished to welcome you to our small village. Please, go sit by the nearest the window and allow the sea air to calm your racing heart. I'll be there momentarily." She turned then, and Batair walked away to find the table of which she spoke.

He sat and picked up the sheaf of hard paper in front of him, turning it over and back. If he were home, he would have procured his own food or dined with his family on fish and crustacean, then drank the honeyed *kiptluk* they all enjoyed, aged to perfection.

Already he missed his home, but he was here to find his mate. He could wait.

Lifting his head, he enjoyed the air through the window. The ocean called to him, sang to him to come home, to protect and keep. He smiled, sending his love back to it and to his people. Then his belly growled, and he turned to see the woman, Bridget, gliding toward him, a shark among the tables and chairs, platter in hand. He had no idea what she held, but his mouth watered in anticipation.

"Batair, I don't know what you've had for breakfast or even what you had last night."

He groaned. Last night, he'd snacked on fish left in the fridge and had choked down water. The fish wasn't fresh, and the water was filled with chemicals that turned his stomach.

She continued. "I remember when Kamau first arrived and the descriptions of what he enjoyed, so I've prepared a little something for you." She set the platter down, and sitting on a bed of sweet brown seaweed was fresh lobster, large fish eggs, and a small bowl of soup. He looked up, knowing his heart was in his eyes.

Bridget's smile was warm and tender. "Eat, Batair. But remember you are surrounded by humans. Pull back your teeth, and while your eyes are a thing of beauty, they will terrify my other clientele."

Batair noticed then she was right. Already, he'd failed. Set before him was food he craved. His stomach growled louder than a walrus, and parts of him had shifted almost immediately.

Bridget reached out a hand and gently stroked his cheek. "Don't worry. Kamau had to adjust when he first visited. You will, too."

Batair took a deep breath and assumed his human appearance. Kamau and this place. How had he survived here? Well, he'd had Bridget—that was obvious. And he'd had his friends.

What had it been like for Kamau at such a young age to arrive at a place surrounded by humans to live a portion of his life with his human father? For the rest of them, all they knew was their brother was gone for a time only to return less happy, less himself. That was, until he shared stories of Bridget and her sisters and then later friendships he'd formed during surface living. Then, one day, their mother's eyes were shining with happiness for her traveling siren. Kamau had found his mate, the one who would support him, love him, and make him laugh. Someone to make his dwelling a home.

Batair had asked for the same opportunity then. He wanted what his brother had, his own mate, a person to come home to whom he could share stories of his battles. Batair could picture them swimming together over ocean volcanoes, taking in the rush of the sea turtles as they migrated, and showing him his world. Batair would share his life. He had only to find him.

16

In the meantime, though, he stayed at the restaurant, ate food that rivaled his home, and watched. Sometimes Bridget sent him on errands, forced him to make deliveries where he spoke to others, engaging in conversations whose topics were foreign to him. He visited the store Kamau shared with him, a market, and with help from Iona, another of the Sisters Three, and Louis he'd purchased food and clothes and learned how to exist as a human.

At night, he returned home to his empty bed.

But he was hopeful. It would only be a matter of time, Bridget told him.

"How do you know?"

Bridget would smile that slow, calculating smile, the one that lit up her golden eyes, then squeeze his hand.

"Patience, guardian."

He shared knowledge of this woman with his mother, and she just smiled. It was almost as if the two of them worked together.

"Patience, Batair."

It was enough to drive him out of his mind. He searched and looked, sent out his own power to no avail.

When the salted shower of Graham and Kamau's home was not enough, Batair would venture out late at night or early dawn, when no one was around. He went back to the ocean, allowed the sea to embrace him. He would release his human features, don his scales, and allow his tail free to slap against the waves. It was a chance he took, he knew, but he was careful. He missed his home.

He had been in the surface world two weeks when the earth shook.

CHAPTER FOUR

Aoki stumbled forward, his lungs stretching with each breath, his skin crawling to get near, to find the scent, and to claim. He was overwhelmed, but the ancient dragon within pushed him on.

"Fucking. Interfering. Conniving. Shit." He wanted to scream at his mother. Aoki knew she had something to do with this. Flames were tearing over his body, his wings beating beneath his shoulder blades, but he couldn't turn while his dragon fought him to get to what was in that restaurant.

Treasure. His dragon's roar, the intensity of its need threw Aoki forward. He barely had control of his own limbs, the power of his movements taken over by the dragon. The closer he got to the restaurant, the stronger the scent became, and with it the blood rushing through his veins stormed through him, threatening a shift.

It had been a while since he'd flown among the clouds, his wings spread wide as they beat against the breeze. But the relaxation that came with a shift, the joy of soaring high, wasn't a consideration presently. Aoki needed what was beyond those doors.

Slamming them open, he twisted his head back and forth searching for his prey, for what belonged to him. A figure sat in the back, tall and hulking, his body covered in strapping muscle, and the shirt he wore worked to contain his bulk. His skin was a burnished gold, and when he looked up, he had the greenest eyes Aoki had ever seen. He'd painted eyes like that before, had seen eyes like that in his

18

dreams. Eyes the color of seafoam, brilliant and shining and directed at him.

Treasure, his dragon bellowed.

The man rose then, and his arms reached out. Tall did not cover the breadth and width of him. How had he entered the door of the restaurant? Why was he here? How could Aoki get him out of here, into his home, his bed, beneath his body, screaming on the end of his cock?

Aoki stepped forward, and the giant's eyes widened, and Aoki could see the confusion. He smiled, but he knew the grin he wore was dangerous, a twisted curve to his lips that had caused others to step away in fear. Not the stranger, though. Not his.... What was he?

The man moved forward. "Mate?"

Mate. Aoki ran the word over in his mind as he approached nearly within touching distance. He would be able to run his fingers over all of that skin and muscle.

Mate. His dragon pulsed with joy, the happiness within a living, breathing thing that twisted in his soul.

Mate. His heart thundered, and he turned around, forcing himself to run away, throwing himself through the doors and out into the waiting sun.

Aoki heard the steps behind him, and chairs being thrown left and right as they slid across the floor. He turned to see that they barely missed Iona and a small family as they entered. When his feet touched the soil, the earth tried to capture him, force him to be still, but he sent his own surge of power and tore his shoes away. He was near his car in seconds, nearly buckling the metal in his desire to get inside. Pulling the door closed behind him, he pushed the button, rejoiced at the sound of the car starting, backed up, and spun around.

He was there, the man, his arms wide open, his fingers toward the sky, the clouds darkening in the distance. His

lips moved, and Aoki didn't have to have the window down
to hear what he said.

Mate.

He got the fucking hell out of there.

* * * *

Batair returned to the restaurant, his heartbeat so loud he
could hear it in his own ears. His mate. He'd seen him, had
almost touched him before he'd spoken, and the creature
had taken off as if a battery of barracuda raced after him, his
black almost blue hair flying behind him.

His mate was slim but not skinny. He was tall, not as tall
as Batair, but then no one Batair had seen so far was as tall as
he was. He was a guardian, after all.

And he was glorious.

His mate.

His smell had been different though, not human. More.
And his eyes. Purple eyes so vivid and intense, eyes that
crawled all over him and seared his flesh with their need.
Batair ached, his dick hard beneath his pants. That same
need stirred him, made him breathe harder, squeeze his
hands into tight fists as he helplessly watched his mate drive
away.

Bridget neared him then. He knew her scent and realized
it was like his mate's, different but not.

She turned to him. "Well, as the first meet for my son, this
was better than I expected." She reached up to him, her hand
gently petting his cheek.

Batair looked down and welcomed the reassuring touch.
"Your son?"

"Yes, guardian. Aoki is my son and your mate. We only
have to convince him of accepting that."

Aoki. My mate's name is Aoki.

Batair looked back toward the road where Aoki's car had

nearly taken flight. "Such fire and spirit. He's a jewel among men."

"Darling. Aoki is not just a man. My beautiful boy is a dragon." She turned away and called back over her shoulder. "Come. Have a cup of tea with me."

Batair didn't want a cup of tea. He yearned to find his mate, hunt him down and stake his claim. Aoki. The name stormed through his soul — and he was Bridget's son.

If he were preparing for battle, he would gather all the knowledge he could, then go to war. It made no sense to go in blind. So, though he wanted nothing more than to follow the fleeing Aoki, it was better he discover why he'd chosen to run.

"Have a seat, Batair. I have a story to share."

The other sister, Cara, dropped off a cup of tea. The scent calmed Batair from where he sat. Bridgett thanked Cara before she eased away, her black and silver streaked hair catching the light.

"I don't need your enchanted tea to be calm, Bridget," he said.

Bridgett nodded, then took a sip of her own cup. "Just a little something to soothe the nerves, but I understand your need to always be in control, guardian. However, this time, you may need to give up a little of that power you grip so tightly if you wish my son's hand to be there instead."

"Riddles. Speak plain. And your son. Did you know?"

Bridgett looked at him, her eyes sparkling. "Of course I knew. I had to be certain you were who Aoki needed. And you are."

"How do you know this?" Batair wasn't sure he liked being tested, that all this time the witch knew who his mate was and said nothing. He sipped his tea and waited.

"Did you think when I sent you to help families, to run errands that I was not learning about you or your character?

You are new to living away from your ocean, but that has not stopped you from offering aid to others, from lending a hand. Even if you're not sure how to approach a runaway four-year-old so close to the cliff's edge, you did."

There hadn't been a thought. Batair had been sent to deliver a meal to a whiplash-tongued woman, her eyes snapping fire and her patience short. He'd stood while she told him about having to raise her daughter's children, about how tired she was, and it was too much for a woman her age to take on. As if to prove her words true, the little urchin flew out of the door and took off, his tiny legs pumping fast and hard. Batair spun to chase, the woman's screams in the distance.

Batair had kept running, admiring the boy's speed as he pursued. The child stopped and turned, his grin wide and challenging. He leaped into the air, his fists pumped in victory, but then he stumbled. Batair's heart dropped for they were at the edge of a cliff, far out from the woman's property. Batair called the wind at the same time he rushed forward and grasped the child's flailing hands. The wind cradled the shaking child, who seemed to finally realize how close he'd been to falling. Batair lifted him in his arms and was grasped tightly around the neck. He carried the little warrior home to the boy's tired grandmother.

When he returned, there were tears on the grandmother's cheeks, and she was so grateful. The boy only had sisters, no brothers, and he was the youngest. He was lonely, and with Batair standing there, he'd seen a chance to play. So, Batair had gone back once or twice to do just that, and young Caleb had been happy. Martha, his grandmother, lost a little of that whiplash tongue and smiled when Batair came to visit.

He looked at Bridgett and nodded. "You said you had a story to share."

"I do, and it may help you understand Aoki's hesitation." She sighed. "Years ago, I fell in love with a dragon, Aoki's father, Katsuro. It was a quick love affair, and before I knew it, I'd had a child. I hadn't known that my dragon lover had a world he had to lead beyond the clouds, one that wouldn't welcome a human mother and her child—especially a witch. I hadn't known his responsibilities, the duties he held. To keep us safe from harm, he left us, so none would learn of our presence. He visits me, but he has never tried to have a relationship with Aoki, who's wanted nothing but a father since he was a little boy."

"You're his mother. Why didn't you insist his father take on the responsibility of caring for his own child?" Batair thought of Kamau and Graham and their pod, of the way Kamau tended to his mate. He thought of Kamau's pain when Graham suffered, and the joy that lit his face when they were all together. He wanted this, and it angered him that Aoki had also wanted but had not received it.

"Because, unfortunately, guardian, I am not perfect. I love my dragon, and when he comes to me late at night or early morning, after months of being apart, I find myself too weak to resist. I believe him when he says Aoki's life would be in danger were he to acknowledge their bond, but this has damaged my beautiful boy's trust and made it harder for him to accept someone of his own." She looked at Batair and added, "I'm hoping with you this might change."

CHAPTER FIVE

"Fucking hell! She knew! Damn it!" Aoki slammed into his home, the solid oak door doing nothing to shut out the feeling of having his mate within his grasp. A mate. Fuck. He didn't want him, didn't want to remember the scent of the ocean wafting from his skin, or to see the lines of his magnificent form begging for his touch. How dare she? He'd told her, made her promise. But she'd never actually promised, had she? His mother had only said she would not control his decisions, not act against him.

Somehow, she would try to prove to him that she wasn't at fault, that she did not make this happen. But she'd called, asked him to come, and his mate had been there.

Against his own wishes, Aoki wondered about his mate—the tall, beautiful man strapped in solid muscle, with eyes the color of dark cyan. The man who looked at him with surprise and wonder filling those orbs. Aoki could paint them from memory alone.

Aoki's dragon stormed beneath his skin, restless and angry. He could feel the wings pressing against his flesh, eager to erupt, but he would contain him, hold him back. Aoki had no doubt that if he were weak even for a second, he would shift entirely and his dragon would search every hidden corner of Charleston until he found the treasure he sought.

Mine! The word thundered in his soul, but he wouldn't listen, wouldn't accept it.

"No," Aoki shouted, throwing his keys down and wrapping his arms around his body. "No." If he held himself together physically, perhaps he could stop the need crawling along his entire frame, the twisting of his insides as he warred with his own creature. "You will not!"

Mine! The battle began anew. Aoki gasped, falling into his favorite chair, seeking the comfort of familiarity, of safety. This was his den. He was safe here. He pulled the blanket he'd left on the floor over him, trying to ignore the trembling. The scent of lavender rose from the fabric, and he breathed it in, trying to find the usual calm it brought him. He closed his eyes and envisioned full lips needing to be kissed, a golden neck that pleaded for his mark. Aoki's dragon roared.

Aoki gasped as pain spasmed along his back, the ache recognizable. He often welcomed the way his body would change and the release he would feel as the dragon tore from his core, wings raised and ready. This time, though, he would be stronger than the instinct that fought him. His eyes watered as he clasped his hands tighter, but the skin had already begun to transform and darken, the scales sliding over his hands.

He could control this, could ease the dragon, but the energy had never been this unyielding before. He breathed through the struggle, the pulses of air leaving his mouth like the sound of a freight train. His chest rose as his back bowed, slivers of agony tearing him apart, but he held on. Instead of the claws that had erupted through flesh, fingers appeared again, the scales became translucent and then disappeared.

The word *mine* grew quieter, but Aoki knew this wasn't over, that he would have to be vigilant. He hadn't wrestled against his dragon since he was a child—when the ancient creature that shared his soul sought his freedom and won. He'd return to his mother, her eyes wet with tears as she and her sisters scried for him, her hands raised skyward seeking her son within the beast.

Aoki had grown up learning control and techniques to calm and ease his dragon. This time, though, he knew it would only be a matter of time before he lost the battle. He heard the echoing chants of *mine, treasure, and mate*. He felt the need to find the man, whose name he still didn't know, but for now, he was calm.

When Aoki stood, his knees nearly buckled, but the more he walked, the steadier he became. He would go paint tomorrow. He wouldn't take the chance of leaving the house tonight. He walked down the hall to his bedroom where he would rest.

The next day Aoki went to his studio. He hadn't rested well at all, dreams of his mate startling him awake... often.

Aoki loved his studio, found peace there. There were days when he would finish painting and then take to the air. It was nice that his studio boasted a large window and a balcony where he could leap out and sail on the wind. Aoki loved his house. It was his solace, his sanctuary, the only thing that gave him comfort, even if there were many nights that he felt alone.

Shaking off the sadness, he picked up his easel, his paints, and his portable stool. Aoki nodded at the humming he heard within his body. *Ease*, he sent to his dragon, but he was ignored. His heart twinged painfully, but he ignored it. He packed his things and went down the stairs to his kitchen to grab a few drinks and a snack. To appease his dragon, he placed raw meat in a sandwich bag.

"There now," he said as he popped a piece of the flesh into his mouth and all but heard the smacking of lips and felt the lick of a forked tongue. He was forgiven, but only a little. It would take more to placate the beast that roamed his soul, but the meat would have to do.

More. Aoki smiled as he ran the blood over his teeth, then shut the door behind him

Be good, and I will.

He felt the growl as he walked to his car.

It didn't take long before Aoki was sitting on his stool facing the ocean. It had been a while since he'd been here. Weeks, maybe. It was funny. He was not an ocean person or even beast. His dragon took to the sky, enjoyed fires, especially the ones he created — before he learned how to control that, too. But the ocean seemed to call to him. He marveled at that.

As Aoki sat sketching the sea, his mind went back to the encounter at the Sisters Three, to the man with the green eyes who stared at him in shock and called him *mate*. He could imagine that man in the ocean, a part of the life there. Aoki recalled the scent of salt and sea that surrounded him. Before he realized it, he'd already worked the man's likeness into the sketch, the water flowing against him, crashing over his shoulders. Naked. Aoki wondered what he looked like naked, what his nipples tasted like, how his skin would feel beneath the palms of his hand.

"You've captured me there on your canvas."

Somehow, Aoki wasn't surprised to hear that voice, had almost expected it. His dragon craned his head toward the sound, its immense body moving, turning.

"You're hard to forget," Aoki said grudgingly.

"And why would you want to? No other has before."

Aoki growled at those words.

My treasure, Aoki's dragon roared, his anger at anyone who would dare to touch his possession thrumming through Aoki's veins. The need to shift, to protect, and to eviscerate any challenger beat against his psyche. Aoki took a deep breath, put his pencil down and turned.

No, the man hadn't changed. If anything, he was more stunning up close. The confident smirk that twisted those full lips that Aoki wanted to claim and see wrapped around his dick. He was taller than Aoki. Aoki stood at 6 feet, but this giant, this larger-than-life man, towered over him.

The stranger's arms were magnificent chiseled rocks of granite that Aoki could imagine wrapped around him. And his body was its own work of art. The mediums Aoki could use to render his flesh on his canvas, or to immortalize him in sandstone or marble? His mouth watered at the thought. Even more than that was his dragon's need to possess, to shift until he was large enough to carry his mate away to his den beyond the mountains—and keep him—thundered in his soul.

"Mate."

"I have a name, jackass," Aoki said.

"From your tone, I would assume this is not an endearment... the word jackass." The man stood closer, and Aoki shivered while his dragon purred. "I am Batair. And yes. I know your name, Aoki. But it is not the only name that I think of when I see you, when I stand close enough to touch, to taste." Batair touched him then, wrapped those granite arms around Aoki and brought him close. Aoki couldn't deny that he lifted his chin, his lips at the perfect angle to accept Batair's kiss.

Moonbeams and stars. Gold dust and diamonds. The first taste of his favorite ice cream, or the rush when a painting was complete. The way his wings embraced the wind when he took flight. All of these things poured through Aoki's mind as Batair kissed him, dipped his tongue between Aoki's lips, and gripped him tighter against his body. His own hands erupted into claws, and he slid them up the shirt Batair wore, slipping down his body and digging in.

Aoki heard Batair's gasp and felt the strength of his dragon pour through him, nearly lifting them both off the ground before he came back to his senses.

"Aoki," Batair whispered while he licked his lips, then bent and traced his tongue over Aoki's neck.

Aoki groaned and tried to regain his control, but the feeling of being just where he always wanted was too potent, drugging. His dragon had no such misgivings. No, he wished to reel Batair in, to let him think he was in control before his dragon captured him forever.

"Mate," Batair whispered hungrily.

Aoki growled, and ignoring his own needs, he stepped back away from Batair. "I have a name, Batair. Use it. I am more than your mate."

Instead of becoming angry, Batair's smile deepened. "Ah, then you agree you are my mate?"

Aoki threw up his hands and turned away, but his blood thrummed with the need to have Batair beneath him, to claim what belonged to him.

Gentle hands rested on his shoulders, and a soft voice whispered in his ear. "It would seem there are things I must learn, my..." Aoki's shoulder's tensed, and Batair changed words, "... Aoki."

Aoki relaxed minutely, but it was enough to give Batair permission to draw closer, the heat of their bodies aligning, as Batair continued his whispered words. "I would be honored if you'd teach them to me that I might have the chance I have often dreamed of. To grow closer to you."

Aoki turned then, and beautiful eyes observed him carefully, waiting. His dragon purred within, its long tail uncoiling, its body pressing against the surface. "I have a life here." He did. He taught art to students who needed him, even if his favorite student was moving away and the ones behind made him wish he was the one leaving. But it was his life, what he'd known, and what he'd made for himself. Aoki knew being with Batair, exploring this bond, would change that.

More importantly, it would change him. And then where would he be? Left behind, or perhaps he would be doing the leaving. Dragons didn't stay, didn't love the children they left behind or mend the hearts they broke along the way. Though he was half human, he knew many of his instincts were governed by his scaled beast, gifted to him by his father's blood.

"I have a life as well, responsibilities to my people. It would be my dream for you to see my home, travel with me."

To see Batair's home would be more than a quick drive, Aoki bet, but he felt the yearning, the need to be with Batair. Still, he had his own home, his own life, and he didn't need a mate to complicate it.

Batair's eyes warmed, the green vivid as he focused on Aoki. "I am asking for time with you, Aoki. Will you grant me this?"

CHAPTER SIX

Batair watched as Aoki's thoughts flitted over his face. He stood there, a guardian of Neptune, asking another for time. If he wished, he could simply take Aoki, drag him across the sand to the ocean. He could hear the song of the ocean, the request to come home. After his conversation with Bridget, he knew ripping his mate away from the life he'd built for himself would not endear him to his mate. If Batair he wanted Aoki—all of him—he had to leave behind the urges to demand and control.

So, he waited, gritting his teeth inside as he resisted. And maybe there was a rightness to what the witch had said, because Aoki looked at him then, the fire smoldering a little less, his body losing some of the rigidity.

"Yes."

One simple word, and Batair's joy blazed across his soul. *Yes.* "You will share yourself with me?"

Aoki's smile was wicked, a sly thing that slid across his face and turned up the heat around him, if that were even possible with the way the summer sun was cooking them both. "Yes, Batair. Parts of me."

Batair moaned, surprising himself with his own need. He shook his head and reached out to Aoki, who moved forward into his embrace. It was a marvelous feeling holding his mate, the length of Aoki against his body. Resting his chin on top of his hair, Batair breathed in the smoky incense of Aoki's skin. He listened and heard the rumble Aoki's chest made, the sound of his dragon.

31

Should I confess to Aoki I know about the creature that shares his soul — know why he is so hesitant to find love? Or let him tell me that himself?

"I'm hungry."

"I am, too." Batair smiled, sliding his hand down Aoki's body, resting his fingers at the top of his shorts, ready to slip them inside to touch Aoki's warmth.

"Not for that. Food, Batair."

"Sex with you would nourish me."

Aoki groaned.

Batair laughed. "Fine, then. What is your desire, Aoki? What would give you sustenance?"

Aoki looked at him, a smile in those eyes rather than the earlier anger. "A burger."

Batair sighed. "Oh, charred animal flesh. Of course."

"Not a fan?"

No, Batair was not a fan. He enjoyed his meat pulsing with life as he tore into a fresh kill. He couldn't wait to savor a meal at his mother's table surrounded by his brothers and sisters.

For now, though, he'd enjoy this time on the surface with his mate, eat food that was not killed by his own claws or those of his family and friends. He would sit, watch his mate eat, struggle to swallow whatever was present and be grateful.

"No, but for a moment with you, I will," he sighed. Aoki grunted and moved out of Batair's arms to gather the elements of his craft. "Have you always painted?"

Aoki looked back at him, a brow raised. "You honestly wish to know."

"Yes, Aoki. I would know everything about you."

Instead of answering, Aoki turned back to his task, taking out a cloth to wipe his hands. From the many drops of paint both old and new decorating the shorts he wore, he could have just wiped his palms over those. Batair would have enjoyed the sight of him bent over, the curve of his sweet ass in the air.

It appeared as if Aoki scented Batair's need. He raised his head into the air and turned to Batair, his purple eyes—so like his mother's—turning black as midnight. Batair shivered from the waves of want that slammed into him, his knees almost buckling. Aoki was suddenly there, against him, broader and intense, his fingers sharp as claws at his back and positioned beneath Batair's ass.

"Everything?" Aoki asked. The word a growl that rumbled from his chest.

"Yes," Batair responded and heard the breathlessness in his own voice. He should be ashamed. He was a guardian, not a seahorse. But the intensity with which Aoki looked at him, the fire he felt, made him tremble. Aoki grinned hungrily, and his teeth were jagged pieces of ivory, sharp and dangerous.

He watched as Aoki struggled, confusion dancing over his face, but in moments it was gone. The black slithered out of his eyes, the purple hue returning to them. The smile was gone, replaced with a look that was more human, less animal. Batair was disappointed. He'd liked the fire that blazed there, the way Aoki had nearly lost control. But he said nothing.

Aoki turned to finish gathering his things, his back rising and falling, an indication that he was struggling. Batair could hear those deep breaths he took.

"As long as I can remember." Aoki was responding to Batair's earlier question. "I've never needed anything more than to bring visions to life. With my art, I can."

"May I see your other paintings?"

Aoki finished packing and turned to hand his easel to Batair. "There. Make yourself useful. And... maybe someday."

"At your command, my mate." Batair bowed his head

slightly. Aoki groaned, but Batair only laughed and followed him to his car.

Later they sat at a restaurant that Batair had never visited before. It was different from Sisters Three. It was small but overflowed with a sea of people who chatted and talked and laughed as they waited for orders to be filled. For Batair, it had been a struggle to walk through the door, his shoulders almost too broad for the frame. There were a few places to sit, but the standing crowd left barely room for a man of his size to move around. Batair was uncomfortable but didn't complain. He made certain he kept a watchful eye on his mate and followed his round ass as he cut a swath through the people on his way to the back.

When they were seated, Batair's bulk precariously resting on a chair across from Aoki, he breathed deeply, and the scent of his mother's table washed over him.

"Neptune's Balls! What is that?"

Aoki laughed. Picking up a menu, he handed it over to Batair and took one for himself. "The smell of delicious food. Look through your menu. There's nothing on it you won't enjoy."

Aoki's laugh was a siren's call, alluring. It trapped Batair in its song, and he found it hard not to simply sit there and beg for it to continue. Instead, he opened the menu, surprised to see dishes that would rival those of home. Flayed lobster with fat, round eggs swimming in buttered sauce teased him from one of the images, while another showed a mackerel, the organs intact with seasoned sea vegetables and potatoes. Batair's mouth watered.

"The food here is fresh. The burger that I plan to have is bloody enough to satisfy my inner monster."

His dragon. Of course. Batair looked at the pictures, read through the descriptions. When he'd decided what he would order, he looked up to find Aoki studying him, and the need to touch and taste overrode his system. Before he could say anything or lean forward into Aoki's space, the waitress appeared to take their order. She looked at Batair, her blue eyes widening, her hand shaking as she wrote. There was fear there, and Batair had no idea why.

He didn't know the girl, but then the more he looked, the more he recognized... something. She took Aoki's order, her ease with his mate obvious, the tension leaving her shoulders immediately.

"Still practicing your art, Coralia?" Aoki asked.

It was exactly the right question, because instantly Coralia told him all about what she'd been doing lately, asked advice and her cheeks warmed with pride. Aoki asked to see pictures, and Coralia turned to Batair quickly as if to ask for permission. Strange. It was the custom of a servant in a restaurant, though. Nothing out of the ordinary, right? Batair nodded, and Coralia turned back to Aoki and pulled out her phone.

"They're beautiful, Coralia. Your grasp of color has improved. I can picture myself there."

Batair had to see what made Aoki's face light up with pride. "May I look, Coralia?" Her name, so like his people at home, was easy on his tongue. She turned back to him then.

"Of course, g-, sir," She blanched, then held the phone out to him, her hand trembling as she did. The image on the screen was of his home, not his specifically, but this woman, this creature had painted the water dwellings, the bubbles, the fish and sea life that existed, and the gardens. How? He looked up at her, truly looked and immediately she backed away.

"Your work is as beautiful as Aoki says, Coralia. May I ask you something?"

Fear lit her eyes then, but she nodded quickly. "Yes."

"Where did your ideas come from?"

"Coralia!" someone shouted from the kitchen. When she turned, there was no way Batair could miss the tracing of gills along her pale neck.

"I'm sorry. My father's calling. I'll get your order in." She pocketed her phone, picked up the pad and pencil, and ran to the kitchen.

"Always in a hurry from the first day I met her."

Batair looked toward the kitchen where the sea creature had fled. His people. How long had she lived here? Who was her father? Her mother? As far as he knew, Kamau was the only one who'd been given permission to remain on the surface. There were stories of others, though, rumors of people who'd fallen in love and decided to live in the human world, hiding their existence. Was Coralia one of those, her parents?

"Batair?" The worry in Aoki's voice broke through his thoughts, and he turned back to look at Aoki. "Are you okay?"

Batair smiled. "I'm fine."

He reached out his hand and grasped one of Aoki's curls, and gently pulled him closer. Aoki's moan was decadent, the growl beneath that even more so. He kissed him, running his tongue along Aoki's lips, and Aoki pressed for more. Satisfied, Batair leaned back and chuckled when Aoki followed him.

Aoki shook his head as if he'd been drugged, tracing his tongue along his lips.

"More?" Aoki's eyes turned black, and the smirk Batair wore slid away.

"Aoki?"

Aoki's smile was slow, his teeth sharp.

"Yes more," Aoki growled, and the voice wasn't his own.

Batair's dick went rock hard, and he could barely breathe. His chair moved as he was pulled forward, his chest slammed against the hard wooden surface. His head rocked back, his neck vulnerable to claws that cupped his throat. "Soon, treasure." Something licked along his throat. "Mate."

"Aoki," Batair gasped, unable to move.

"Batair? Do you need something to drink?"

Batair was suddenly free and shaken. He reached to his side for his weapon, some way to protect himself, but he saw that Aoki's eyes were gold, not black, his smile sweet, not dangerous. Besides, he had no weapon here, no trident. No dagger at his side. And the way Aoki looked at him—as if he had no idea what had just happened—was chilling.

"Drink. Yes, a drink would be lovely." Something intoxicating, because he was going to fucking need it.

He watched as Aoki stood and went to the counter— nothing different about his walk, the way long legs moved beneath a tight ass. He wanted to palm his cock as Aoki leaned forward to get them a drink, laughing with Coralia, who glanced at Batair and then away.

When Aoki returned, he handed Batair a bottle, the cap already off. "Coralia has to leave and run some errands for her father, so we'll have someone else as our waiter. She's a busy girl."

Batair nodded and took a drink. It was pleasing but lacked the fire he enjoyed. It would only slake his thirst.

He glanced to where Coralia had disappeared. There was something strange there with Coralia, something that bore looking into, but that was for later.

Batair was more concerned with bottomless black eyes and being held captive. Aoki's dragon had not hesitated to stake its claim. It was the human he would have to win, though.

Batair set the bottle down, and Aoki cleared his throat.

"So."

Batair lifted a brow. "So?"

"What has my mother told you?"

CHAPTER SEVEN

Holding his dragon back was harder the longer he and Batair sat together. The blank spot in his mind worried him, especially the moment his thoughts cleared to see Batair's head back, lips open, and his breathing labored. But then he snapped immediately forward, challenging, his hand at his side.

If Aoki had brushes and a canvas, he would have painted him then, his warrior, alert and ready, weaponless but undeniably powerful.

He waited for Batair's answer. He couldn't imagine his mother leaving out any details. Her need to see her son married off and happy was always first and foremost in her mind. The fact that her son was half dragon, a possible roadblock for anyone with a good head on their shoulders, would be shared quickly to get the ball rolling.

Batair looked at him warily, anticipating what, Aoki had no idea, but he leaned back finally and appeared to relax, his ocean green eyes flickering over Aoki before he cleared his throat.

"You are not fully human."

Aoki sighed. No, his mother did not disappoint. "No, I'm not, but then neither are you."

Batair smiled, and Aoki could see the sharper than normal teeth, the lovely curl to lips he craved to bite. And those eyes. He felt his dragon rumble within and shook himself.

Batair laughed softly. "No, I'm not, and it is good you know this. I would hate for you to be disappointed. Before you sits a guardian of Neptune, leader of his forces." The words were stated with pride that appeared arrogant.

"You say this as if it is important." Aoki knew it was, but the look on Batair's face at his statement was priceless. The way his eyes brightened as if challenged, the flare of color that blushed along his skin a thing of beauty.

"Of course it is. We are the front line, at the ready if an enemy should press their advantage. The guardians obliterate any challenger to Neptune's throne. You should feel honored for me to be your mate."

"Oh, honored because you come from a line of people who hide beneath the ocean waters? Those who don't know the world they live in?"

Batair actually growled, and Aoki's dick hardened. The wave of energy that rose from Batair excited him and made him want to reach out and pull the guardian against him, his claws at the back of his neck, his neck vulnerable to his bite. But Batair was in full snit, his eyes so green they shined with an inner light that blazed.

"Guardians do not hide, little dragon, and neither do our people. We are masters of the sea, not hidden away beyond the clouds hoarding treasures, afraid to reach for more than we can see."

It was like a bucket of ice water had been thrown at him. Hidden beyond the clouds? Yes, that was where his father was, in the mountains with his people, high above the world around them, only venturing out when they felt there was the opportunity to attain more. Then they dragged their new possessions back to the mountains. Aoki didn't want that life, never had.

He'd never been given a chance at that life, though. According to his mother, his father was protecting him, sheltering him from those who would feel threatened by a human who had ties to the dragon world.

No, instead of a father who adored him as he saw those around him loved and protected, he only had his mother and her sisters. Not even a grandfather. There was perhaps a teacher or two who had taken him under their wing with encouragement as he grew to manhood. Yet he'd never tossed a ball back and forth, gone fishing, or done any of things fathers did with their sons in those Hallmark movies he pretended not to watch.

Aoki looked up at Batair, who glared back at him. "No, you're right. Dragons do hide away, hoarding treasures and giving nothing in return. Maybe you need to keep that in mind in your desire to have me as your mate."

Batair would have spoken, Aoki could see the words forming on his lips, but a new server appeared. The tray he carried was laden not with gold and diamonds but with bowls and plates overflowing with steaming food that neither he nor Batair had ordered. But the way Batair's eyes brightened with joy, Aoki knew he'd brought him to the right place.

"My father sends these dishes he says would please you, sir," the young man said as he placed the plates on the table.

Plates of tentacles surrounded by oranges and other types of fruit, a bowl of berries and fish, another bowl of frothy foam that hid little bits and pieces of something, as well as a platter of seasoned meats surrounded by thin sheets of seaweed and fish roe. The last thing was the hamburger and fries that Aoki had ordered along with his favorite mango lemonade.

Batair looked at all the food and back to the boy who stood there waiting. "Please relay to your father that I am grateful to sit at his table and would lay my trident at his feet, my conch shell in the palm of his hand if I had them. That I am at rest." The boy smiled, the white of his teeth as sharp and as startling as Batair's own.

"Thank you, sir. I will tell him."

"Please ask him to stop by. I would be honored to meet him." When the boy hesitated, Batair went on. "I only wish to see him, to share a word. That's all." The boy looked back at the kitchen nestled away in the back and turned to Batair again. "Please."

There was a nod, then Aoki and Batair were left alone again.

Batair looked at Aoki. "Thank you." Batair's eyes were warm, the green heated. He reached out and opened his palm, and hesitantly Aoki placed his own hand inside. "Thank you."

"You're welcome, Batair." Aoki cleared his throat, then removed his hand. "Let's eat."

The food was good, but sitting with Batair, watching him devour the plates of food before him, was even better. Aoki watched stunned as tentacles disappeared, as whole oranges were ripped apart and their juicy bits savored. The shiny wetness on Batair's lips proved a temptation Aoki was finding hard to resist. Fucking food porn, it was. And so unfair.

They spoke while they ate, with Aoki sharing parts of his life, his joys, and hopes that he'd given to no one else. He wasn't an open man. He generally kept to himself, enjoying his solitude, something he was sure was passed down from his father. But here with Batair, he felt free to share.

Aoki shared his desires to open a youth center for budding artists, a safe haven for children like Elizabeth Ann McCormick, where they could go and not feel the burdens of their home environment. Instead, they would have somewhere their talent could flourish unhindered by unreasonable expectations and the traumas forced upon them.

Sitting with Batair, whose eyes focused on him, who listened intently, and smiled with pride at his future plans, made his heart beat faster and anticipate things he tried not to want.

"It is unfortunate that this haven you desire should be on land alone. I know of children, little ones who would certainly benefit from care such as this. The sea is abundant in its offerings of beauty and life, but it can also be dark and cruel, where that life is taken without mercy. Land dwellers are not the only ones who have pain." Batair looked toward the kitchen and back to Aoki.

Perhaps it was a ploy to return him to thoughts of becoming Batair's mate, but Aoki didn't think so. The sadness in the depths of those green eyes hurt Aoki to his very soul.

"What about you, Batair? What do you dream of, what do you wish for the future?"

Batair's eyes widened in surprise. "No one has ever asked me this. What I want? I am a guardian."

Aoki dabbed at his mouth and leaned back. "And what does that mean? A guardian?"

Batair's eyes lit up at that. "I am born to lead Neptune's army, to fight from the front lines beside the sirens."

"Siren. That's what Kamau is."

Batair smiled. "Yes, my brother was born a siren. It is a noble position, but not one that confines him to the sea. He has the freedom to roam, but he is one of many sirens. While his talents with music magic are without question, he is not the only one with them, but he is one of the greatest born. Guardians are born to remain beneath the waters, to fight in times of battle, to grow stronger and train those that come after. I am the greatest of my kind, my light shining the brightest of them all. My brother and I are a formidable team."

Batair was proud of this. Aoki could see it in the way his chest rose as he spoke. The scent that emanated from him was potent, and Aoki could feel how aware his dragon was, how much in need he was to claim this for his own. But this was not the time. No. He wanted to know more about Batair, not just spear him with his cock, wrapping those muscular legs around his body as he took him. He shivered.

"So, that is your dream then? To fight for Neptune. What's it like to know a God, anyway?"

"A God? Hmm." Batair lifted a glass of amber liquid to his lips and drank. "Oh, this is divine." Placing the glass down after another healthy swallow, he continued. "No, I am a part of Father Neptune's line. He is my grandfather."

"Grandfather? Then that would make you how old?"

"Old enough. The years below don't pass as quickly as they do here, hence Kamau's ability to visit and seem new. It does mean that he and Graham must remain longer beneath the surface. Should they not, then Graham will age as his human brothers and sisters do on land." Batair took another drink. "As for knowing Father Neptune, I follow him and lead the others. My life is forfeit if he desires. No, don't look like this."

Aoki had no idea what may have crossed his face, but there was rage burning within him, his dragon's need to protect coursing through his veins. His skin itched to stretch, to accommodate his size.

"It makes me happy to see your desire to protect me, but Father Neptune loves me, and would not take my life without true cause. I am faithful in my duties to him, work unerringly to support my people and to protect all. I train with the thought of pleasing him. It is ever present in my mind, the core of my existence. I am fine, my mate. My dragon."

Aoki growled then, ready to drag Batair off, but a shadow crossed their table, and they both looked up to see a beautiful golden man, whose hair was tied back, the ponytail holder surely struggling to contain the mass of hair it held.

"Guardian, I hope your meal pleased you."

Batair's welcoming smile immediately calmed Aoki, the joy of it so bright it could have lit any dark room. Batair stood and took the stranger into his arms hugging him tightly. There was a moment, a small one, where Aoki thought to separate them, to shift his human hand into his dragon one and use his ebony talons to severe the man's neck, but he took pride in his ability to control the urge. So, he took deep breaths and waited.

When they separated, Batair placed his hands on the man's shoulders, shoulders almost as broad as Batair's. "You are a guardian."

"I was."

"Was?"

"Yes. It is a long story, but now I am just a father raising two children. This is my restaurant, my home is within walking distance, and my family is safe." There was a warning there, and Aoki wondered if Batair heard it as he did.

Batair nodded. "You would not be here were it not Father Neptune's wish."

"Yes, but then I no longer care what he wishes. I am simply grateful that he leaves me be. Still, it is nice to see someone from home. There are times when I wish to visit, to see my people, but the pain is too great to return. I've chosen to live here above the waters of the ocean until my children are strong enough to return to the ocean with me, should that ever happen." Aoki saw Batair look beyond the man to see the boy who served them watching.

"I would hear the story that causes this pain."

"Perhaps one day, but that is a story for another time. Instead, I will leave you to enjoy your time with your mate. The way he looks at me could prove dangerous for you." The man smiled, a sort of smirk very like Batair's. "I must return to my kitchen. You will come again?" Aoki saw it then, the need for friendship, for someone to speak to. And that someone was to be Batair. But Batair was his. He wouldn't share him.

Wait, where did that thought come from?

He'd only just met the man. Yet the truth was staring him in the face. Batair was his. And what was he supposed to do about that?

"My mate and I are newly met. Yes, I will return, as this is his home, and he says that this is his favorite restaurant. It is now mine. Your name?"

"Lanh."

Batair waited, but Lanh said nothing more. "Of what pod?"

"None."

"But—"

"None, I no longer speak of the pod or of any members thereof. To land dwellers, I am Lanh Seamus, the name I took the day my children and I arrived here. That's all I wish to be."

Batair's eyebrows creased, and the tightening of his lips indicated he wished to know more, but even Aoki could ascertain this was not the time. He needed to intervene.

He yawned loudly. "I'm tired, Batair. I don't have class tomorrow, of course, but that doesn't change the fact that my body remains on school time." He gritted his teeth but let the next words come out anyway, "Perhaps you could make arrangements to meet with Lanh another day."

It was a relief Lanh that turned his way. It was uncanny both the similarities and the differences between Lanh and his mate. Larger-than-life, solid and densely muscled they both were. While Batair's eyes were a bright green, Lanh's eyes were sea-glass green. Both men were sharp, their skin fitting over their bones in places that looked almost armor-like, but the rest of it was smooth and touchable.

Aoki desired to touch Batair. Hell, he craved to taste him, too.

"Yes, that sounds good," Lanh said. He offered his hand then, and Batair took it. "The meal is my gift to you... brother. Please pass this way again."

Batair nodded. "Thank you, Lanh. I will."

"Aoki, my youngest says you work at her school."

"Yes, I do."

Lanh nodded. "She wanted to be in your class, but learning is hard for her and her time is better spent on her core studies."

Aoki nodded, but he didn't agree. Children needed the arts, needed an outlet.

"Tell her to drop by sometime. I'll be happy to work with her, perhaps after school when her core subjects are finished?"

"Perhaps."

Well, he'd offered. He'd see what would become of it. In the meantime, it wasn't quite a lie that he was ready to go home. "Batair."

"Yes, I'm ready."

CHAPTER EIGHT

The walk to Aoki's home was filled with anticipation. The lithe young man beside Batair was quiet, as if mulling a thought over in his mind. Batair tried to focus on this moment, the peace he felt to be walking along the shore with his mate, but there was a foreboding sense of uneasiness in the air, a peculiarity that made him wary.

He was out of his depth here. If he were in the ocean, his trident at the ready, he could send his power out, and while Batair wasn't gifted in sound as his brother Kamau, he possessed enough ability in his voice to search. Echolocation was what they called it here. For him, it was a natural part of life.

"You feel it, too, don't you?" Aoki questioned.

Batair wasn't sure of Aoki's meaning. Did he feel the energy that passed between them, the need that vibrated along his flesh at the closeness they shared? Or was it the feeling of danger that lurked about. The eyes he felt watching from the shadows?

"I feel many things. What is it that you feel?"

Aoki paused, turning to look at Batair. "Besides wanting to tear your clothes off, there's something not right here."

Batair gasped at Aoki words. Aoki was much smaller than he, and though he might have the strength of a dragon, there was no way he was a match for a guardian, was he?

"I see the muscles in that brain of yours working over-time, guardian."

It was the first time Aoki had used the term. Rather than

48

animosity, it was said with unexpected friendliness.

"Can you?" Baltair asked.

"Yes, and I have much to think about myself. Perhaps we can talk about that. I almost hate to admit it, but I enjoyed dinner, spending time with you."

Aoki's smile was devious, like a sly dragon. Batair thought back to earlier at dinner with the creature skulking beneath Aoki's psyche. It had made his blood race, but it had also been as erotic as hell. He craved more of that.

"Maybe, just maybe, mind you, we can do a little more of that. My house is just down this way." They were walking past a line of old trees, ancient if Batair had to guess, and filled with magic that had survived centuries.

"Did your mother choose this area for you?"

Aoki laughed. "Funny you ask. But yes. As with all things she has her hand in, it is filled with magic."

Batair nodded, and yet there was a scent that Batair had not known until he arrived in the human world. Smoke. It was accompanied by tension in the air, both steadily increasing his wariness.

"Whatever happens tonight, Batair, I'm not interested in being your mate, in having a family," Aoki said. This time, though, his eyes were elsewhere.

Batair almost told him he could practically smell the lie drifting from him.

He'd seen the way Aoki watched the families in the restaurant. Aoki wanted one, longed for one so badly he couldn't hide his envy. And Batair desired to give that to him, but just as Bridget had warned, it would take time.

"Do you smell that?" He asked instead. A potent smell filled with wrongness. He looked at Aoki who sniffed the air, the angles of his features changing, sharpening. "Aoki?" Batair didn't have his trident, but that didn't stop him from allowing the change to wash over him as he, too, prepared for the unknown.

When they turned to walk into an area where the trees grew thickest, he could see the tendrils of heavy smoke dancing in the air and the torched ruins of a small home left behind. There was only the foundation, the rest of the building smoldering.

Aoki's cry was one of pain and loss, and Batair's heart broke for him. They ran to the home, but there was nothing they could do. There was nothing left to save. All around them the land was charred, as if a coursing flame had incinerated the entire area. There was an odd smell mixed in that hinted at something more than what any accident could produce.

"Everything. Everything is gone. How? Why?" Aoki choked out. "My work. My home. Everything." Aoki turned to Batair. "Did you know about this?"

Batair was shocked. How could Aoki think something like that? Aoki didn't know him, they had only just met. Still, they had been together.

"Me? I was with you. I had nothing to do with this." But he would. He'd find the person that did this, protect his mate. "I would never do anything to hurt you."

Aoki stared at him until he seemed to deflate, the fight in him gone. A beam fell, and the embers flew into the air like lightning bugs, the sound of the charred wood crashing to the ground. When Aoki would have moved closer, Batair held him back.

"I have to see if anything's left." But there was no way there could have been. What had to have been a brick home had gone up like a matchbox. "I had paintings that took me years to finish. There must be something." The pain in those words tore at Batair's soul.

"No, Aoki. There's nothing there."

"But why? Why would someone do this?" It appeared

Aoki suspected this was not an accident as well. "Take away my home, all that I worked for?"

Batair wrapped his arms around his mate, pulled him close to his chest, Aoki's dark head against his body.

"I don't know, but we'll find out. We will."

Aoki's sobs twisted Batair's insides. "I have to call 911, the police, someone." Instead of making a call, Aoki stayed in Batair's arms, his smaller body sheltered by Batair's larger one as he shook.

When Aoki calmed, Batair reluctantly released him to make his call, his fingers slipping on the screen as he dialed the number. Later, the firemen arrived to douse the sputtering flames left behind. When all questions were answered and it was confirmed that there was nothing to be saved, he held Aoki's trembling shoulders as they walked into Batair's home. It was actually Kamau and Graham's, but it was his for now.

Ever since they'd left Aoki's, Batair's mate had been in a sort of daze, his purple eyes haunted, his face bleak and empty. Aoki could rebuild, although selfishly, Batair didn't want him to. He wished for Aoki to go home with him, back to the ocean. But it wasn't time. Not yet. Now, he needed to care for his mate. That was his priority. He tugged Aoki along to the bedroom.

"Everything's so neat here. I have..." Aoki corrected, "... had shirts and pants on the bed, on the chair, hell, all over the floor. I had plates with food stuck to them in the sink, and something growing in the refrigerator that I think was meatloaf at one point, but here? Nothing is out of place."

"Except for me," Batair said. "I am out of place." He hadn't meant to say it, but it was already there. This wasn't his home.

He missed his brothers, his nephews, and nieces, missed commanding his men. He even missed his mother's meddling and his sister's interfering. But this was where his mate was, and this was where he needed to be. At least until he hopefully convinced Aoki to come home with him. What if that never happened, though?

"I'm sorry."

Batair shook himself. Aoki shouldn't be apologizing. "You've done nothing to apologize for."

"But—"

"No, let me take care of you."

Aoki appeared ready to argue, but his shoulders drooped like a wilted flower. Batair bent and kissed him softly, demanding nothing, only offering kindness. Aoki sighed and leaned against him, and Batair smiled. Taking his hand, he led him to the main bedroom.

When they entered the room, Batair turned Aoki to face him. Gently he took off his mate's shirt, lifting it over his head and tossing it to the floor. Next, he unbuckled his pants and drew them down tanned legs, legs he desired to lick and taste. But again, this was not the time. When he was near Aoki's cock, he paused and looked up at his mate, who was watching him, the pupils of his eyes darkening. Batair took in a breath, calmed himself and went back to his task. Finally, Aoki was revealed.

His mate was beautiful. Aoki might be an artist, but he deserved to be immortalized in stone or paint, rendered in a way to be appreciated centuries later. Batair craved to savor him, to run his fingers over that smooth skin, to bite, and to possess. This was the hardest thing he'd ever done—resisting his desires. As a guardian, there was no end to the bodies willing to service his needs. He'd always believed it was his birthright to take what was offered. But no longer. No other's touch would excite him, drive him to plead for a kiss. Just this man.

Batair stood and took Aoki's hand in his. "The bathroom

is this way. Come with me."

It wouldn't take long for the shower to be ready. Batair liked the way his brother and his mate had decorated their home. There were signs of them both here, Graham's need for order, and Kamau's kinship with the sea. The shower was a testament to that relationship. It looked as if it were hewn from rock, a craggy cliff, but there were places where one could actually sit and have the spray from the multiple shower heads hit those sore and tender places. The water itself was salted, and while it wasn't home, it was enough for Batair to relieve the tightness of his flesh, the constant ache from spending so much time away from the ocean.

He pressed the buttons that would turn on the shower-heads and reached in to assure himself that the water wouldn't scald his mate. When he turned, he found Aoki watching him. The vulnerability he probably hid from most people was more than apparent to Batair. But Batair didn't comment on it. He guided his mate and eased him into the water.

"I'll wait in the bedroom for you. There's a towel over here and shampoo here. The towel holder is heated, which is a pleasure if you stay under the water as long as I do." Batair was rambling. He knew he was, but if he didn't keep talking his eyes would travel lower to Aoki's beautiful long and surprisingly thick cock, and then it would be hard to stop himself from reaching out to touch. "So, I'll be outside. Yes, I said this already, didn't I?" He took a deep breath and backed away.

"Batair?"

The way his mate said his name made Batair catch his breath. Here he was, commander of thousands. When he shouted, arms raised in battle or in defeat. Batair yielded to no one. For Aoki, though, he would lay himself at his feet.

"Yes," Batair said, and his voice was little more than a

moan.

"Stay."

Batair swallowed thickly. Could he do what Aoki wanted? Remain and care for his mate without trying to have more, take more? Yes, of course, he could. He wasn't a whale calf. He had control, even if he was barely holding on to it.

"Please?" Hearing Aoki's plea, Batair realized that Aoki thought he would leave. Batair could no more leave this man when he asked him to stay than he could deny he was already falling in love with Aoki.

"Whatever you need, Aoki, I am here to give."

Aoki smiled then, and those incredible eyes of his grew dark as midnight. Batair shivered, but he moved to sit on the bench outside of the shower.

"No, Batair. In the shower with me."

Batair licked his lips. "Aoki."

"Please, Batair. I just had my home ripped away from me, the only place that I've ever felt safe other than in my mother's arms. I don't know why, but with you, I feel safe. I need you with me. Will you deny me that?"

No, Batair wouldn't. He moved back to Aoki, who stepped further into the shower, the water streaming over his skin, his dark curls falling around his face. Batair toed off his shoes, unbuckled his pants and let them fall. He took off his shirt. He did all of this while Aoki studied him, the flame within his eyes growing steadily, stroking Batair's body without his mate laying one finger on him. He looked down at the underwear Louis had helped him purchase and was glad he had when Aoki's eyes admired the fit, his tongue peeking out between his lips, lips Batair wanted to kiss again. "Hmm, those are quite nice on you, Batair."

"I'll have to tell Louis thank you."

Aoki's eyes blackened at those words, and he growled. "No."

Batair smiled. "No?"

"No one else should see you, see what's mine."

His mate was possessive, over him. He didn't know if it was the dragon speaking or Aoki. From the way Aoki seemed to grow in moments, he was guessing the dragon. When he moved to step back, he was captured, strong hands on his arms, his body slammed against Aoki's chest.

"You are taking too long." Aoki's growl was arousing.

"I am?" Batair questioned. He was playing with fire, but he was willing to be burned.

"Yes. I need you in here. Now." Batair went to remove his underwear, but he couldn't move. Instead, Aoki held him tight with one arm while he ripped the fabric away with the other. "Batair," he growled, again, and Batair's dick grew so hard it hurt.

"Let me take care of you, Aoki," Batair said, then sighed hungrily when Aoki squeezed him tightly, licking and nipping before letting him go.

Yes, Aoki was taller and broader suddenly, and Batair found he liked it. Liked the way Aoki could manhandle him, the way he pushed him against the wall.

"Do it now then, mate. Kneel."

Batair fell to his knees, the salty water pouring over him. He felt himself shifting in answer to his mate's dragon, felt the ridges rising beneath his skin, the widening of his skull, and his fins itching to come forth.

"There you are, beautiful guardian. My guardian." Aoki drew his hands over Batair's head, down his cheek and pushed a finger into his mouth, pressed it against his tongue. "I want this mouth on my dick. I want you to open wide and let me drive into you."

Batair growled, his need to serve his mate overwhelming his senses. "Yes, Aoki."

This wasn't him, was never him. He did not kneel. He did

not beg. He did not open his mouth and swallow as another man's dick was shoved to the back of his throat. He did not groan in pleasure as his face was fucked hard and brutally, fingers gripping his skull to keep him there.

Yet there he was, at Aoki's mercy, being taken, used, and loving it, loving his mate. When Aoki shook, Batair placed his hands on his trembling thighs, legs thicker, more muscled than they had been moments ago, and held on. Aoki roared, and Batair rejoiced in the salted gift from his mate who still shoved, still grunted, who fucked his mouth without mercy, groaning as he flooded Batair's throat.

"Good, so good, Batair."

Batair moaned, drunk off his mate's taste, barely able to stay upright. In fact, he fell forward, his eyes closing.

"It's okay. I have you." Batair barely heard Aoki's words. He moaned as he felt himself being lifted from the shower floor and placed on the niche in the rocky shower wall.

"I don't know... what's..."

"Stay there, Batair. I have you."

"What's going on? I feel..." He felt hot, on fire, like a flame was tearing its way through his body.

"Beautiful Batair." His lips were kissed, gentle and tender. "Beautiful mate. I had no idea, but I do now. We will finish this."

"Aoki?"

Batair blazed with need. He was inflamed, and nothing could douse the fire, at least not the water against his skin. No, if anything, the water was like little blades slicing away at him, his flesh was so sensitive.

"My mother warned me, but I promised myself this would never happen. No one made me feel, made me want, until you."

"Aoki? Father Neptune, what's going on with me?" Batair ached, burned. He needed relief from whatever was coursing through him.

"Then I saw you and knew that you were mine. I didn't want this, though. I didn't. I didn't want to be my father, mate someone, then leave them because of some greater treasure somewhere else, off on some stupid motherfucking mountain when his son needed him."

Batair felt the scream starting in his chest. What was Aoki talking about when he could barely breathe, his thoughts all over the place? "Aoki? What is happening to me?"

"I needed my father just as my child will need me, but I will be there." Batair's scream erupted. "It's okay, Batair. I have you. My mother described this to me, the need, how nothing would take the pain away but her mate."

Batair heard the water turn off, felt the air around him cool, but he couldn't move, not on his own. He was dying, when he'd just found his mate.

"No, Batair, you're not dying." Had Batair actually said the words aloud? "You're in what Kamau called his elustra, but it's altered by me, your mate." Batair was lifted, his large body sheltered against a body even larger than his own. "My dragon has been pushing this, and I emptied my essence into you before I could gain control. Now, we must complete the mating."

Batair felt cool sheets against him, but it was too much and not enough to ease his suffering. Elustra. He barely remembered it. Kamau had described the feeling, the inability to stop himself, the need to mate overwhelming him, but nothing had prepared him for this. "Aoki?"

"Yes, Batair. I'm here. I won't leave you. I don't think you realize how much your life is going to change, but I'm ready to help you, to be what you need, to be who we'll all need. I think I've always been ready."

Batair's legs were stretched open, his knees pushed back, and he felt something wet push into his hole. Aoki's tongue.

"Oh." He screamed again, but it wasn't enough. His dick was hard, leaking, but he needed more.

"Mm. You taste good, Batair. Salty, like the ocean, but sweet, too. I can't wait to stretch your ass with my cock, to drive into your warm body, savor it all."

Batair twisted, flames tearing up and down his body. His fingers were claws, black and guardian sharp. He heard the slurping at his ass and moaned. Aoki lifted up. "Look at your eyes. So beautiful. Mine. To have you wish to care for me, then hear that someone else has helped clothed you... Seen what should be mine..." Aoki's growling grew louder.

Batair tried to explain to him that Louis hadn't seen him, that they'd gone into the store, and he'd looked at him and guessed the size he'd need. But words were lost to him, only moans and pleas, his body writhing in a passion filled agony.

He heard a sound, then felt a chilled wetness poured over the crack of his ass. "We'll need help to get me in there, but you'll rest when this is done, as your body adjusts. It will be fine. I'll be here."

"Please, Aoki." Batair needed Aoki inside him, not talking, not humming comforting words, heated whispers in his ear, but inside him. "Please, Aoki." Then Aoki was there, and Batair howled long and hard, wrapped his legs around Aoki's waist and held on as his mate thrust inside him, his length spearing into his ass without apology, his arms locked around Batair's shoulders with no space between their bodies.

"Mine. My mate. Inside you. I can already feel the change, the *more*." Aoki pushed harder, and Batair screamed for more, more, more, roaring loud as his ass was taken and stretched, molded to his mate's cock.

There were tears in Batair's eyes, his heart filled with love for the man that moved above him claiming his body and soul, ramming into him again and again.

"Yes, I feel it, feel it coming. Do you accept me, Batair?"

Batair moaned, his mind crazed with need as he waited for his mate, waited for the next step in their lives. "Yes, Aoki. Everything. I want everything."

"Good, because it's here." Aoki lifted then, pulled back and then shoved himself in as far as he could until Batair swore he could feel the tip of his cock in his throat. "There. There we are. Good. Welcome us."

Batair's hole stretched as seed greater than what had filled his mouth earlier poured inside him. The fire that blazed over him slowly faded as more and more cum flooded inside, but Aoki didn't stop, only kept moving, keeping himself lodged inside Batair like a cork in a wine bottle. Batair groaned as Aoki rocked above him, stretching him, rotating inside. When Batair came, he all but blacked out, the pleasure of his mate spilling into him too tremendous to ignore.

Aoki kissed Batair on his forehead, on his cheek, down his neck, then Batair felt sharp teeth at his throat.

"Batair?" Aoki asked, and Batair said *yes* without hesitation, gasping as those sharp blades sank into him, warm lips surrounding the spot where they pierced. He moaned as he listened to Aoki drink.

When he finally closed his eyes, he sighed. Aoki's hand slid gently over his belly as he turned them so that his dick didn't leave Batair's body.

"There you are, my mate. I'll take good care of you, good care of us all."

CHAPTER NINE

Aoki was leaving this city, leaving Charleston and moving to the ocean with his mate, a mate that he thought he would never have, never know. A mate who didn't know yet that he carried their child in his belly, that Aoki would watch him with joy as his belly rounded. Aoki would watch as Batair lost his guardian rigidity, laughing instead, smiling as he and Aoki prepared to spend their life together.

Aoki had his own family now. A new subject for the new artwork he would create. He hadn't been able to save a single painting from his home, but there were a few he kept locked away in his classroom that now shared space on the walls of his temporary home. It would do until he could add to them.

"Aoki," his mate called, having come in from a run along the shore. Weeks after their initial mating, Batair didn't run quite as fast anymore. In fact, he was breathless. Still, Aoki said nothing. He listened to him move about while he sat on the couch and channel surfed. He was a little afraid his strong guardian, *born to lead Father Neptune's forces,* would lose his mind if he told him. Aoki was a coward, hoping Batair would figure it out on his own. From the conversations he overheard between Batair and Kamau, he wondered if Kamau suspected what Aoki already knew.

He enjoyed looking into the circle Batair created to talk with Kamau, seeing life below the surface. He hoped to paint the children he saw swimming to and fro, and the creatures there. Batair said he would be able to do that, to live a life similar to the surface once they arrived. Like Graham had been granted, there would be areas of air provided, spaces large enough for even his dragon to roam free.

Tonight, Aoki planned to present his mate with his true form. They were going to the mountains today to ensure that he had space. He wanted to feel Batair's hands on his shoulders, his legs pressed against his wings. To fly, carrying his mate on the wind.

Batair had asked several times where they were going, but Aoki said nothing, only smiled and said he had to wait. When his mate would have argued, he kissed him sweetly and marveled at how his touch affected Batair. It was a blessing that he wouldn't take lightly.

"Back so soon?"

"Yes, I don't know what it is. I'm hungrier, and yet I exhaust so quickly. I think it's life here." Batair placed his hand on his belly, cradling it protectively. "Whew. I could eat a whole octopus. I want to go to Lanh's place later. I told him we'd drop by."

Soon. I'll tell him soon.

"Maybe when we get back. It might be late, and we have a long drive." He smiled at Batair. They'd fucked this morning and again before Batair left for his run. Seeing his mate growing with his child only made him want him more. He heard the rumble. Obviously, his dragon agreed.

"Well, when do we leave?"

* * * *

Batair sat on the grass of the mountainside Aoki had brought them to. He felt captivated and free. Aoki sat nearby, painting and laughing as he told Batair several times not to move. How could he not move? He felt something new on the horizon, a new life where he wouldn't be alone anymore.

If he was honest with himself, he was ready to move on, to leave the life of the guardian behind him, to enjoy his mate and their future. He had responsibilities, though. He had to remember that. But those thoughts were for another time. He smiled at Aoki as his mate sat on a chair with a new easel and new paints they'd bought while shopping in North Charleston.

"If I could, I'd paint you instead," Batair said as he moved yet again, much to Aoki's consternation. He'd already threatened to spank Batair, and he found he warmed at the idea of Aoki's hand striking his ass.

"You would? And how would I look?" Aoki asked.

"Well, you'd have beautiful lilac eyes that glowed on the verge of blackening, like when you want to fuck me. Curly brown hair that fell past your ears. An athletic body that looks amazing in a pair of tight jeans."

"What if I were a dragon?"

Batair paused. "A dragon?"

"Yes, what if I took off my clothes right here and changed just for you? What would I look like then?"

Batair's eyes were wet. "You'd be amazing."

Father Neptune, what is wrong with me lately? Batair had no idea. He'd spoken to Kamau about it, about the changes he was feeling, but Kamau knew nothing. Graham, though? Graham just smiled slyly in the background, then picked up their youngest and laughing as he walked away. When he asked Kamau what was wrong with his husband, Kamau had choked and closed the circle.

He didn't care about any of that. His mate stood before him naked, and Batair wanted to crawl on his knees to him and swallow his dick, but he didn't. No, he watched as his mate grew, stretched and arched his body, his skin coating over in scales, his muscles expanding, his legs shifting until a black and red dragon stood before him, iridescent scales dancing along his body, black tipped claws at the ends of his arms and legs.

Aoki was massive, colossal, and he had wings. Wings! He trilled to Batair, and Batair stood immediately. He walked to Aoki and reached out his arms, and his mate nuzzled his chest, pressing his crown against him.

The dragon turned around, and his huge tail barely missed striking Batair to the ground. Aoki turned his head when his back fully faced Batair and called to him again.

"You want me to ride you?"

That shrill sound had to be a yes. Batair went to his mate, ran along the tail and wrapped his legs around the space between the wings. He held on, his fingers tight on the base of the wings. When he was settled, his dragon flapped his impressive appendages and was off.

It was the most breathtaking feeling Batair had ever experienced. The way Aoki flew among the clouds, racing the birds beside him, dancing on the wind, was awe-inspiring. He was flying. Flying! His mate was a dragon. He was in love, and he was flying.

They went high and spun, and Batair held on, laughing as they flew. Aoki drifted for a time, then dove towards earth only to spiral out and fly up again. And Batair rejoiced in it all.

When they finally touched the earth, Batair's mind was spinning, giddy, and happy. He slid from Aoki's back only to have his dragon charge around in front of him, screeching loudly. Immediately alarmed, he turned to see what was wrong.

"So, the little hatchling has grown up and found his mate, has he? Too bad, he won't live long enough to enjoy his new-found family."

Batair spun, trying to see beyond Aoki's shoulder, but it was nearly impossible. All he could glimpse was a dark headed man wearing what appeared to be a blue gown of some sort. It didn't matter, though. Whoever this was had threatened his mate. He needed to fight. He moved forward, intending to slide beneath Aoki's right leg, but his mate wrapped him up in his tail and lifted him off the ground.

"Aoki! Let me go!"

Aoki turned and roared at him. "You can't do this alone."

"Yes, Aoki," another voice, this time a woman's voice said snidely, "Let him go. You cannot fight all three of us. Release your little mate."

Batair heard the third one roar before changing instantly into a dragon, its size almost as large as Aoki's own.

"Daiki, I wished to play with them."

The golden dragon turned to her, roaring a command. The woman who wore a green gown shifted, becoming an emerald green dragon, the snarl of derision easy to find on her lips. She stalked forward, trapping Aoki and Batair between them. Batair squeezed at Aoki's tail.

"Let me go, Aoki."

Aoki mewed, but Batair continued. "I was born to fight, mate. Let me help us!"

Before Aoki could answer, one of the dragons struck, its claws sinking into Aoki's chest, dragging his mate across the ground.

Batair fell, but he was ready and rolled away, releasing his human self, his entire body covered in armor from the crown of his head to his webbed feet. Claws pushed through his fingertips, and his eyes sharpened, allowing him to see in the darkness around him as clearly as if he were in the sea.

He roared, and the winds changed, answering his call, the earth beneath his feet rocking. They were near the ocean, and she knew his voice. He leaped into the air, arms raised, and attacked the dragon who held his mate. Using one arm, he gripped him while the other arm became a blade. When he thrust it into the dragon's neck, the blood was like acid smoking over him, and if he were human, he would probably have lost that arm.

But he wasn't human. He was a guardian. He tore his arm away and pulled the head of the dragon off with it, laughing as it fell to the ground open-mouthed in shock.

Aoki fell back then, breathing heavily.

"It's okay, mate. I have you," Batair said before he dropped to the ground and a shadow rose over him. It was the green dragon, wild and screaming. The sneer was gone, replaced with rage. She opened her mouth, and Batair knew what was going to happen. The bitch was going to burn him — or try. He lifted up and crawled back to get away, but she placed a clawed foot on him to trap him, and then the fire came. It was hot, hotter than hot, but Batair only felt the heat. He didn't burn. It did nothing to him. Still, it wasn't comfortable, and the ground around him began to smolder.

He twisted, moving in vain. If he could grip something, anything that wasn't on fire, but he was suddenly free. When he looked up, the green dragon was gone, and Aoki stood in her place, blood dripping from his lips. Batair looked around to find the female dragon wounded but not dead. She rose again slowly, prepared to fight.

The other dragon, the one in blue charged forward then, and Batair struggled up quickly, ready. He shifted the other arm into a blade. No, he didn't have his trident, only himself, but he wasn't powerless. He raised his arms to the sea and knew she was ready if he needed her.

The female stood, and together the two dragons ran toward Aoki and Batair. Aoki was not trained to fight, not as Batair was. That didn't matter to him apparently, because he didn't hesitate. He lifted his wings and rose, rushing toward the battle.

"Stop!" A voice shouted, loud and commanding. "Stop!"

The two dragons turned toward the voice, instantly falling to the ground. Aoki spun and twisted, and if a dragon could look shocked, Aoki certainly did.

He shifted then, and Batair opened his arms to catch him, embracing him tightly before putting him behind him to keep him safe.

"You see what has happened, Taka! In your eagerness to cleanse my home, you have lost your lover. He lies dead while you stand here wounded and torn. And your foolish brother? Will you bring him to his death as well? Because I promise you, mistress, should you and your house come near my son and his mate again, I will destroy you."

"Father?" Aoki questioned. Batair turned to his mate and wrapped his arms around him. Aoki held on tightly, weak, as if he was struggling to breathe. "He's here."

"Yes, Aoki, I am here, my son. I am only sorry that it took so long for me to realize what a fool I've been."

"Yes, my mate, but you only hoped to protect our son." Aoki's mother walked forward, her arms outstretched before her. Bridget chanted softly, and the body of the dragon rose and twisted, lifting into the air, its head following.

"Take your mate's body back to your lair, Taka. Allow your home to see what was done," Katsuro said sadly.

The female dragon roared again, and the other dragon looked up and then over to Aoki's father. Taka stepped forward, but suddenly a purple dragon stood in front of them all. He roared once and flew to her, knocking her to the ground. She was under him, powerless to move, unable to free herself as Aoki's father tore into her. She cried out, begged, and then she was human.

The other dragon went to help her, but the ocean, tired of not being in the fight lifted over the edge of the land and dragged him into the sea.

Aoki's father shifted, covered in Taka's blood.

He took a deep breath and wavered, and Bridget ran to him, holding him tightly in her arms. He sighed and kissed the side of her temple.

"I think now would be the time to talk, Aoki," Bridget said.

* * * *

The tea was good and not spiked with his mother's herbs, so there would be no spilling of truths involuntarily. Batair sat next to Aoki while his father sat across from him, his eyes watching every movement he made, taking him all in. He was clean, the blood washed away, and dressed in a linen gown, brown with a large medallion over his chest. His hair was shorter than Aoki's, but Aoki felt as if he were looking in a mirror. He hated it. It was the one fear he battled daily, that he would grow up to be his father, deserting those who needed him.

"You know, I'm not one of your treasures. In fact, you never treasured me at all," Aoki said bitterly.

Katsuro took a deep breath. "I only look at you, son, because I regret the time I've lost. You were always my treasure."

Batair's hand tightened around Aoki's own, giving him the strength he so desperately needed.

"I only stayed away to keep you safe, to let you grow up without the dangers that surround a child of the *Yosumi*. I've listened to your mother's stories about you, watched you from a distance. Sadly, it was my following you that allowed Taka and her house to hunt you down." Katsuro's purple eyes were sad, but he smiled at Aoki, hopefully. "There are four houses, Aoki, that rule the dragon kingdom. Families given the power to make decisions, keep traditions that should probably have died out a long time ago. This was done centuries before my time to maintain the balance so that if one dragon's greed overrode his good will, his ability to lead fairly, there would always be another to cleanse the house that had been judged as *Horitsu Ihan*, breakers of the law."

Katsuro looked at Bridget, who entered the room, and instead of choosing the seat beside him, she sat in his lap, making herself comfortable. Immediately Katsuro calmed, and he wrapped one arm around her tightly. "I fell in love with a beautiful woman who challenged me, told me where I could go the first time she met me. How could I resist such a gift? I had to have her."

Bridget sighed, then kissed Katsuro's cheek. "But I'm human, and a witch."

"This is true. To mate with a human is one thing, but to have that woman also be a witch? It was breaking *horitsu*, the laws that governed our dragons. What if this human, this witch, were able to convince me to do things, to commit acts that would endanger the dragon realm? It was not to be. Knowing this, I visited your mother in secret, hiding our bond and then hiding our child, not just from the other houses, but from even myself. I've regretted this every day of my life."

"But you've changed? Now?" Aoki was skeptical. All his life, he'd wanted his father. What made now different? There was so much time lost.

"I learned that Taka's house had been given the task of cleansing mine. It was done without my knowing, a meeting that occurred in secrecy. They followed me, the last time I went to see you and realized that my son had found his mate." He looked at Batair then. "You are worthy of my son, Tetra Batair. To see the way you fought even when he tried to keep you away. Thank you."

Aoki watched to see if Batair was shocked at the use of his

full title, but he showed nothing.

"There is no need to thank me. I love Aoki, would give my life for him. Instead, we will share it."

Bridget looked at Aoki and then at Batair. Her smile was mischievous. "Oh, my beautiful guardian. That's not all you'll share."

"Mother," Aoki warned. Of course, his mother would know. "Let me."

"Okay, Aoki. But I've waited my whole life for this."

Batair looked from mother to son, confused. "What's going on?"

Aoki was quick to answer. "Nothing." When Batair didn't look satisfied with that answer, he squeezed his hand. "Please, Batair. Let my father finish."

Katsuro gasped, and Bridget leaned against him. "Yes, you heard him. He said father, now finish so we can finally begin planning for our lives together rather than apart." Katsuro's eyes were wet when he looked at Aoki's mother, eyes filled with love. After a brief kiss, he turned to Aoki.

"I've ended our house. I no longer wish to be a part of the dragon realm, for our family to be trapped in the past. I want to live with your mother and to know my son. I told the other houses this. They accepted my choice, but the Nakamura house was unable to call back their assassin. Taka had made it her mission to destroy my house. By the time I'd learned of this, your home was burned down. Gratefully, I arrived in time to stop Taka only to learn that my son's mate had been chosen well, and he had his own protector." Eyes the color of amethyst, so like Aoki's own, looked at Batair. Katsuro bowed his head slightly.

"So, you'll live with my mother?"

"I will."

"What about Taka's house, the others?"

"Since their desire to cleanse my house went against the

decision of the others, their house is no longer sanctioned to rule. It will take time, but another house will be chosen to replace both of ours. I'm sorry for Taka's grandfather. He's a good dragon, but he was unable to control his house, so now it is lost to him. In refusing to listen to him, Taka has destroyed everyone connected to her, even her mate." He looked at Bridget. "I will not make the same mistake. I choose my mate, my son, and to have the life I've always desired." He looked at Aoki. "I will even visit you in your new home if you will allow it."

Aoki should be angry, should deny himself the relationship his father offered when he'd needed it so many years ago. Instead, he turned to Batair. "Would I be able to communicate with my father through the circle?"

Batair nodded.

"Yes, I would like your visits, but we can talk and see each other through Batair's circle."

"I'd like that, Aoki."

Aoki's throat was full of tears, but he refused to cry. "I would, too."

EPILOGUE

David and Louis stood next to Batair and Aoki. David looked at Batair. "You look different." His finger was on his chin, his dark hair in his eyes as he studied Batair.

"I don't stare at you nearly as much as my husband, but I agree with him. You look different."

Batair had to agree with them. Not only did he look different, he felt different. He was no longer tired. No, now he was ravenous. Lanh often joked of how he would devour the entire restaurant if he could. They laughed, but Batair was starting to worry. If he were home, he could visit the nurturer, see what was going on with him. Was this what happened when a merman mated a dragon?

"Yes, but I'm not sure what it is. You're not sick. In fact, you look quite healthy. So healthy. So very, very healthy."

"David," Louis warned.

David laughed. "Just explaining, darling. Anyway, your face is changing, and don't get me wrong, but you've put on a bit of weight, too. In fact, if I didn't know better, I'd swear—"

Aoki was quick to interrupt "Okay, Batair. We have to talk. David and Louis, you have to go home." When David would have argued, Aoki growled, "Now." David shook his head, while Louis smiled knowingly and dragged his husband along.

Within moments, the two were gone, and Aoki turned to look at Batair.

Though he was worried a little about Aoki kicking David

71

and Louis out, Batair couldn't believe how lucky he was. In days, he would take his mate home with him, where Aoki would teach, where they would blend their lives together. They would someday have a family. He looked forward to having children with his mate. The idea of being a father made him happy and had been the center of his most recent conversations with Kamau.

Aoki came to him and took his hands. Batair went to him, immediately. "I have something to tell you."

"Tell me?"

"Yes, let's sit down." That was another thing that was getting harder to do. There was a pressure inside, something he'd never felt before. He really needed to see the nurturer.

Aoki helped him to sit, and Batair took a much-needed breath. "Okay, my drake. What is it?" Perhaps if he contacted Kamau through the circle tonight, he could ask him to bring the nurturer too, maybe get some advice on what could be done. They would leave in a week, but he was beginning to think getting some help would be better now than later.

"I may not have had a connection with my father, but my dragon and I have always communicated. He is an ancient being who inhabits my body, often acting on his own decisions. We are bonded, but he has a mind of his own."

Batair agreed, with a smile. There were many nights where he and Aoki made love, only to be awakened by the dragon half of Aoki ready to mate again. Afterward, Batair slept long into the morning, pleasantly used, his body wrapped tightly in Aoki's bigger, more dominant half.

"Your body is changing, feeling different?" Aoki asked.

Batair looked down at himself and found his hand around his waist again. For some reason, it made him happy, comforted him to know all was well. "Yes, I feel different. I have no idea why, but tonight I think I'll talk with the nurturer.

We call her when—"

"You're pregnant, Batair. My dragon mated you, and there's nothing wrong with you other than you are carrying our child," Aoki rushed out.

Batair laughed. Aoki and his jokes. He found his mate had quite the sense of humor, and he enjoyed it. He was living. He was happy. It was all he'd ever yearned for. But Aoki wasn't laughing. There was no twinkle, no sly smile.

This wasn't a joke.

"Pregnant." Batair looked down again at himself. The exhaustion, the hunger, and the pain. He looked at where his hand lay protectively. Over their child. It all made sense. The care from Aoki's mom, the food she brought over, the way Katsuro looked at him, his eyes warm and hopeful.

Inside, he carried a child. Aoki's child. This was wrong, wasn't it?

He looked up at the man he loved, the deepening black indicating they weren't alone, that the dragon was there with them.

His mate waited, nervous, his breaths shallow.

"This can't be. I'm a guardian. You're supposed to carry our child, not me. I was born—"

"To fight? To lead? How about to be more? To be the father our child needs, maybe even raise a future warrior, a painter, or whatever our baby will choose to do." Aoki reached out to Batair. "We are mates, and it was fate that our family would come through you." The heat was there in Aoki's eyes, and Batair was helpless to react.

Aoki kissed him, his neck, licked at his ear, a spot they'd both learned drove him nuts, then pulled at his clothes to get to his skin. When the clothes didn't open quickly enough for Aoki, he tore them off Batair's body. Kneeling in front of him, he rubbed his head against Batair's stomach, because though he'd refused to admit it, he had a belly... one filled with life.

Aoki looked up at him, eyes dark and bottomless. "My mate. Our child." Aoki stood then, and picked up Batair with him, carrying him to the bedroom.

"Aoki?"

"Hmm."

"What are you doing?" But Batair knew, and he would be lying to himself if he said he didn't want his mate's dick inside him, filling him once again. It was funny to realize how happy that made him, to be claimed by his mate.

Aoki placed him on the bed gently and stood back to admire him. "You are beautiful, my guardian. My strong fighter, my warrior. My heart is full when I see you carrying my child inside you." Aoki stripped his clothes off as he spoke, his heavy cock rising. He gripped it tightly. "We will have many children. Perhaps more than Kamau and Graham." He knelt down on the bed and pulled Batair's legs apart. Batair shivered as Aoki bent down, pressing his tongue into his ass.

"Aoki," Batair growled, then moaned with pleasure as Aoki twisted to get more of him.

"Yes, my mate. Father to our child."

"Please."

"Batair, I love you. Do you know this?"

Batair was happy to hear it, to hear the words he'd craved as long as he could remember, but right now, his body was desperate for something different.

"Batair?"

Batair looked into Aoki's beautiful purple eyes. "Yes."

"I love you."

Batair smiled. "I love you, too, Aoki."

Aoki nodded. "Now, open your legs wider. Display yourself for me." Aoki had been asking him to do that more often lately, to present himself before Aoki took him, and it drove Batair insane. Aoki caressed his stomach, bent and kissed him there. "So beautiful, Batair. You are so beautiful." He sighed. Then the dragon was there in Aoki's eyes, present and wonderful. "Our child is within you. Our future."

Batair shivered. "Yes."

Aoki grinned, and it was all teeth. Sharp claws slid along Batair's flesh, opening him, then Batair gasped with pleasure as Aoki's dick surged into him. Thrust after thrust, the bed shook as Aoki took him. Batair's shouts were loud, his gasps and grunts decadent. It wasn't long before he felt Aoki's teeth at his neck, felt the pain as they pierced his throat and heard as his blood was swallowed deeply. Then Aoki was coming, his body shaking as he emptied himself inside Batair, who followed him over the edge without hesitation.

The two of them lay together, Aoki's arm around Batair's waist, his fingers drifting back and forth over his stomach.

"I love you, Batair."

"And I you, Aoki."

"I will never leave you. I will protect you."

Batair knew this was important to Aoki, so he turned to look at his mate. "I believe you, Aoki. More importantly, I believe in us." He looked down at himself and back at Aoki. "I'm not sure what this means for me as a guardian, but I know one thing."

Aoki placed his hand on Batair's belly. "And that is?"

"No matter what happens, or how my life changes. No matter what comes next, you have given me the greatest prize I'll ever know."

Their kiss was sweet, tender, and all that Batair had ever dreamed.

ABOUT THE AUTHOR

Deja Black had fantasies of men loving men, men who felt strongly, loved hard, and needed a hero. Then one great day she came across a book and discovered the world of m/m writing, encountered others who shared her obsession as much as she did, and found a world where she could not only be accepted for the lives and loves she envisioned, but she could create them too. So why not? Why not take the stories she would write and throw away as a teenager, grow them, dream them, and make them a reality where she could know her own characters, let them live their story, and make them real for someone else? And she did. Now, with the support of her hubby and some intense time management, she is learning to balance her family of two children at home and the many others she teaches each and every day with her passion for writing what she loves to read.

Deja is always interested in connecting with new people who also share her love, so please feel free to contact her at:

Facebook: https://www.facebook.com/deja.black.69
Blog: http://dejablack77.blogspot.com/
Email: DejaBlack69@gmail.com